KT-116-827

EGMONT

We bring stories to life

First published in Great Britain in 2009
by Egmont UK Limited
239 Kensington High Street, London W8 6SA

Thomas the Tank Engine & Friends™

CREATED BY BRITT ALLCROFT

HiT entertainment

ISBN 978 1 4052 4420 6
1 3 5 7 9 10 8 6 4 2
Printed in Italy

FSC
Mixed Sources
Product group from well-managed
forests and other controlled sources
Cert no. TT-COC-002332
www.fsc.org
© 1996 Forest Stewardship Council

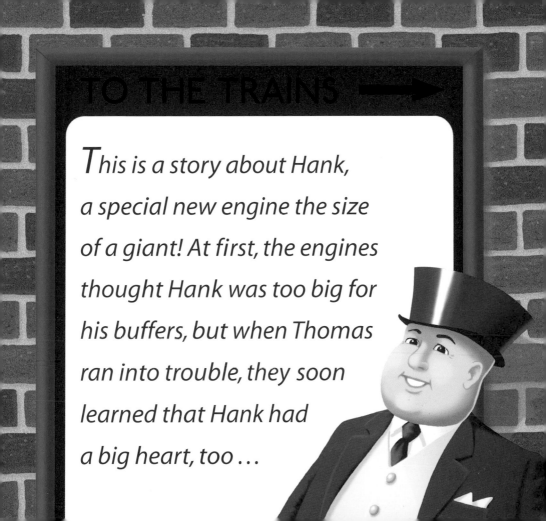

*T*his is a story about Hank,
a special new engine the size
of a giant! At first, the engines
thought Hank was too big for
his buffers, but when Thomas
ran into trouble, they soon
learned that Hank had
a big heart, too …

Hank was a brand-new engine who had just arrived on Sodor.

Hank was very special indeed. He was a very big, blue engine with bright red boiler bands.

The Fat Controller invited all the engines to come and welcome Hank to the Railway. When they saw how big Hank was, they gasped.

"Hank looks as strong as a giant!" peeped Percy.

"I'm sure he isn't stronger than a Sodor engine, though," Thomas puffed, proudly.

The Fat Controller had a lot of jobs for Thomas to do that day.

"First you must take new machines from the Docks to the factory," said The Fat Controller. "Then you are to pick up slate from the Quarry and deliver it to the Shunting Yard. Lastly, you must pick up an old tractor from Farmer McColl's farm and take it to the repair yard."

"Yes, Sir," peeped Thomas.

Hank thought Thomas must be a very important engine to have so many big jobs to do.

Hank was pleased when The Fat Controller told Thomas to show Hank all the sights of Sodor.

"You must be back by teatime for Hank's welcome party at Tidmouth!" The Fat Controller said. "Hank is a very special engine."

As Thomas buffered up to the trucks that held the machines for the factory, Hank chuffed alongside him. Hank wanted to make friends with Thomas.

"Hello there, Thomas," whistled Hank. "You look like the finest little engine I've ever seen!"

Thomas was not very pleased to be called 'little'. "I'm a tank engine!" he huffed.

Hank saw all the trucks that Thomas would be pulling. They looked very heavy. "Let me take those trucks for you!" chuffed Hank, helpfully.

"No, thank you!" peeped Thomas. "I'm strong enough to pull much heavier loads than this!" he said, and he puffed out of the Docks.

Hank hoped he hadn't hurt Thomas' feelings.

Thomas and Hank arrived at the Quarry. Hank was surprised. He was sure The Fat Controller had told Thomas to go to the factory first.

"I'm going to pick up the slate trucks," Thomas huffed.

Hank was worried. The slate trucks looked heavy, too. "Hold your huffing, Thomas!" smiled Hank. "Let big old Hank take those trucks for you."

"No, thank you!" puffed Thomas, politely. "Tank engines can pull very heavy loads!"

Hank followed Thomas out of the Quarry. Thomas was heaving and huffing. Handsome Hank gleamed as he chuffed down the tracks. But poor Thomas was puffing and panting!

Hank saw children waving from the bridges. "Hello, Thomas!" they called.

"Good to see you!" Hank whooshed, happily. "My, Thomas, aren't you going to whistle 'hello'?"

But Thomas didn't have quite enough puff!

Thomas and Hank slowed at the farm, where Farmer McColl was waiting with the tractor on a flatbed trailer.

Thomas was almost out of puff. "Hello, Farmer . . . McColl," gasped Thomas. "This is Hank . . . the new engine on Sodor!"

"That's a mighty fine tractor you have!" Hank whistled, as it was coupled up to Thomas' trucks. Then he looked at Thomas. "Say, you look all puffed out! I'll take the tractor for you."

But Thomas did not want any help.

Thomas huffed and puffed but his wheels hardly turned as he tried to pull away.

"Take the pressure off your pistons," Hank whistled, kindly. "Couple me up!"

But Thomas would not let Hank help him. He struggled on, crossly.

Thomas and Hank passed through a station. Some visitors waved at Thomas, but Thomas had no spare steam to whistle back at them!

So Hank blew a loud, long whistle for them both, which made Thomas even crosser!

Suddenly, there was trouble!

There was a FLASH and a FIZZ . . . a POP and a TWANG!

The loaded train was too heavy for Thomas. He had cracked a cylinder and couldn't move at all!

"Oh no!" Thomas moaned. "Now the deliveries won't be made, and you won't be back in time for your welcome party, Hank! All because I'm not a Really Useful Engine or even a very strong one!"

Hank sighed. He was sad for his new friend.

"I wanted to show you that I wasn't just a 'fine little engine'," Thomas steamed, softly. "I wanted to show you how strong I am. But I need your help now, please!"

Hank was delighted to help. "You give the orders, I'll do the pushing!" he puffed.

Hank coupled up to Thomas. With Hank shunting the train, they delivered the tractor to the repair yard together. The workmen were sorry to see that Thomas had broken down.

Next, Hank and Thomas chuffed into the Shunting Yards to deliver the slate trucks.

"I hope you're back on track soon, Thomas!" called the Yard Manager, as the trucks were uncoupled.

Finally, Thomas and Hank delivered the new machines to the factory.

"Thank you, Thomas!" said the Factory Manager.

The engines' work was done.

Hank proudly pushed Thomas all the way to Tidmouth.

Thomas and Hank arrived just in time for the welcome party.

"Thank you, Hank," whistled Thomas. "Now all of Sodor knows what a strong engine you are!"

Hank smiled. "I know something, too," he said, kindly. "You're the engine everyone cheers for on Sodor. That's really something to be proud of!"

Thomas was pleased. "You *are* a special engine," he smiled to Hank, "and a very special new friend too!"

Two Great Offers for Thomas Fans!

THOMAS & FRIENDS

In every Thomas Story Library book like this one, you will find a special token. Collect the tokens and claim exclusive Thomas goodies:

Offer 1

Collect 6 tokens and we'll send you a **poster** and a **bookmark** for only **£1**.
(to cover P&P)

My Thomas Story Library - Collect them all

THOMAS & FRIENDS

Story Library

Thomas books available to buy online at www.egmont.co.uk

Available to buy online at www.egmont.co.uk
Look out for 8 NEW Thomas Story Library books in August 2008!

Reply Card for Thomas Goodies!

1 Yes, please send me a **Thomas poster and bookmark.**
I have enclosed **6 tokens plus a £1 coin** to cover P&P. ☐

2 Yes, please send me a **Thomas book bag.**
I have enclosed **12 tokens plus £2** to cover P&P. ☐

Simply fill in your details below and send them to:
Thomas Offers, PO BOX 715, Horsham, RH12 5WG

Fan's Name: ....

Address: ....

....

.... Date of Birth: ....

Email: ....

Name of parent/guardian: ....

Signature of parent/guardian: ....

Please allow 28 days for delivery. Offer is only available while stocks last. We reserve the right
to change the terms of this offer at any time and we offer a 14 day money back guarantee.
This does not affect your statutory rights. Offer applies to UK only. The cost applies to Postage
and Packaging (P&P).

We may occasionally wish to send you information about other Egmont children's books but if
you would rather we didn't please tick here ☐